MONSTER ISLAND

By M.M. Eboch

Illustrated by Sarah Horne

Rourke
Educational Media
rourkeeducationalmedia.com

www.rourkeeducationalmedia.com

Edited by: Keli Sipperley
Cover and Interior layout by: Tara Raymo
Cover and Interior Illustrations by: Sarah Horne

Library of Congress PCN Data

Monster Island / M.M. Eboch
(Rourke's World Adventure Chapter Books)
ISBN (hard cover)(alk. paper) 978-1-63430-394-1
ISBN (soft cover) 978-1-63430-494-8
ISBN e-Book) 978-1-63430-588-4
Library of Congress Control Number: 2015933789

Printed in the United States of America,
North Mankato, Minnesota

Dear Parents and Teachers:

Rourke's Adventure Chapter Books engage readers immediately by grabbing their attention with exciting plots and adventurous characters.

Our Adventure Chapter Books offer longer, more complex sentences and chapters. With minimal illustrations, readers must rely on the descriptive text to understand the setting, characters, and plot of the book. Each book contains several detailed episodes all centered on a single plot that will challenge the reader.

Each adventure book dives into a country. Readers are not only invited to tag along for the adventure but will encounter the most memorable monuments and places, culture, and history. As the characters venture throughout the country, they address topics of family, friendship, and growing up in a way that the reader can relate to.

Whether readers are reading the books independently or you are reading with them, engaging with them after they have read the book is still important. We've included several activities at the end of each book to make this both fun and educational.

Are you ready for this adventure?

Enjoy,
Rourke Educational Media

TABLE OF CONTENTS

The Faun's Cave 6

Navel of the Ancient World 15

Lost and Found... 24

What about Monsters? 30

Going Under 39

Dangers on Land and Sea............................. 48

Ancient Disasters.. 58

The Minotaur... 65

Creatures of the Sea...................................... 70

Saving the Day 78

Chapter One
THE FAUN'S CAVE

Grace stood with her father and her younger brother, Jaden, in front of the cave opening. They stared at the triangle of darkness opening into the pale gray cliff. Dad said, "What do you think we'll find inside?"

"It doesn't look that big," Grace said. The top of the triangle was only ten or 15 feet high. They'd gone to a lot of trouble to reach that little hole in the cliff. They'd flown to Greece two days earlier. The previous afternoon, they'd caught a bus from the big city of Athens to a small mountain town. In the morning, they'd taken a taxi, then walked to the cave. Grace had been expecting something more impressive after all that travel.

"Let's go!" Jaden darted for the opening.

Dad grabbed Jaden's shoulder before he could get away. "No running ahead. It could be

6

dangerous." Jaden was eight, two years younger than Grace, and his middle name should have been Trouble. Dad kept his hold on Jaden and went into the cave.

Grace followed close behind. "Dangerous how?"

"Monsters!" Jaden said. "Or ghosts. Listen." He made a spooky howling sound and it echoed throughout the cave.

Grace shivered, but only because it was cold and damp inside the cave. She was not scared, even if it was dark and creepy. "There's no such thing as ghosts or monsters."

"Hold on, let me get the flashlight. Jaden, stay with us." Dad rummaged in his backpack. He pulled out a light and a beam speared through the darkness. Dad shone the flashlight up and around the cave. The small entrance had opened into a large chamber and the flashlight beam barely reached the ceiling. The cave was much more interesting inside than it had looked from the outside!

Dad's voice rumbled strangely in the large space. "This was a shrine long ago, a place where they worshipped the god Pan."

"Pan was the one who had goat legs, right?" Grace said. They'd been reading Greek legends to prepare for the trip. One of the gods had the upper body of a man and the lower body of a goat. He was a faun, like Mr. Tumnus from The Lion, the Witch and the Wardrobe.

"Right," Dad said. They picked their way around knee-high boulders covered in green moss. "To the ancient Greeks, Pan was the god of the wilderness, shepherds, and hunting."

Grace glanced back. The small entrance was a bright slash of light. Otherwise, the cave was dark except where Dad's flashlight hit. "Why would they want to worship here when it's so dark?"

"They probably would have used candles or lanterns," Dad said.

"I like it in here," Jaden said. "It's dark and spooky." He yelled the last word and it echoed around the room.

Dad chuckled. "You aren't the only one who appreciates it. Caves were considered holy places. You can see how mysterious and special they seem. This cave was used for thousands of years. Archaeologists dug here some years back. They found statues, flutes made out of bone, rings, and clay figures. Also, thousands of knucklebones. Long ago, people used bones for prophecy, telling the future."

Jaden laughed. "How did the bones talk?"

"The prophet would toss the bones on the ground. Then he or she would look at the pattern the bones made and decide what it meant."

"That's crazy!" Jaden said.

Dad shrugged. "People always want to know what the future holds. There's no science behind fortune-telling. Still, people love fortune cookies and reading their horoscopes. I guess it's comforting to think you know what's going to happen."

They walked across the cave floor, which was shiny with water in places. Large, lumpy columns of stone rose up from the cave floor. "Stalagmites," Dad said. "They're made when the water drips down over thousands of years. Each drop leaves a tiny bit of mineral behind. Over time, those mineral deposits build up into a column. Don't touch," he warned as Jaden reached out a hand. "You could damage the column."

Jaden sighed and moved away. Dad turned the flashlight to the ceiling. "The ones that hang down are called stalactites. You can remember that because they have a C for ceiling and they hold on tight – stalac-tite. Stalagmites have a G for ground."

He handed the flashlight to Grace. "Let me get my camera and I'll take a picture. You two stand on either side of that column." Grace stood next to a tower of rock that was more than twice her height. She wouldn't have been able to wrap her arms around it even if she'd been allowed to touch it. Dad got out his camera and looked up. "Where's Jaden?"

Grace shone the flashlight all around. No sign of her brother.

Dad took the flashlight and made his own search. "That kid," he sighed. "I can't turn my back for one second. I'll be glad when we get on the boat, so he can't go far." He hesitated. "On the other hand, we'll be out in the Aegean Sea, so if he does go anywhere...oh, boy. Jaden!" His yell echoed around the cave, like many Dads calling at once.

As the echoes faded, Grace thought she heard a whisper of laughter. But where had it come from?

"He must have gone back outside." Dad started

for the entrance. "I hope he didn't get far."

"No, wait," Grace said. "I don't think Jaden would leave someplace this cool. Besides..." She pointed to a darker area on the cave wall, an opening almost hidden by one of the stalagmites. Dad turned the flashlight on it.

Jaden crouched in the hole, grinning. "Got you! There's another room back here, but it's too dark."

"I should have known," Dad said, shaking his head. "We won't crawl through any tunnels today. The guidebook said you need special equipment for parts of this cave. We'll leave that for the serious cavers."

They took pictures before heading toward the cave entrance. The opening shone like a blinding spotlight as they got closer. Outside, the sunlight seemed especially bright. They shaded their eyes for a minute as they adjusted to daylight. "It will take us a few hours to hike to Delphi," Dad said. "Fortunately, some of it is downhill." The family did a lot of hiking back home in Washington State, so they were used to long walks.

They walked along a path through a forest of sweet-smelling fir trees. After the forest, they passed a farm. They stopped for their picnic lunch, sitting on some rocks. It felt like they were on top of the world, looking down on rounded mountains and blue water in the distance.

"I wish Mom and Joy were here," Grace said.

"Me too," Dad said. "But I like spending time alone with you guys as well." Mom and their little sister, Joy, had stayed in France. Mom was a guest teacher at a college for the summer. The whole family got to spend the summer in France with her. Then Dad got a job writing some articles about Greece. He'd taken Grace and Jaden along, but Mom couldn't take the time off. Joy was only two, so this trip would have been hard for her. Plus, Joy had been adopted from China just a few months before. Mom said she was looking forward to spending time alone with the youngest of her three adopted kids.

Grace understood, but she still wished they could all be together.

A small brown goat wandered near them, grazing on the grass. Grace sat quietly, hoping it would get closer. But Jaden jumped up and ran toward the goat. It turned and darted off,

disappearing in seconds.

They kept walking past hillsides where sheep and cattle grazed. They hiked for a long time, stopping to take pictures. In mid-afternoon, they came to a path lined with stones. It was steep, zigzagging down the mountain. Dad went first and made Jaden stay close behind him.

Then they were looking down on the ruins of an ancient city between steep gray cliffs. "There it is," Dad said. "Delphi: The bellybutton of the world."

Chapter Two

NAVEL OF THE ANCiENT WORLD.

Grace giggled. "The what?"

Dad grinned. "Delphi was considered the 'navel of the world.' Your navel is your bellybutton. But the word navel also refers to the central point of a place. So to the ancient Greeks, Delphi was the center of the world. One myth says that the god Zeus released two eagles from opposite ends of the earth. They met in the sky above Delphi."

Grace imagined two eagles flying around the earth. "No bird could really fly that far."

"No," Dad said, "and besides, where would they start? Where are the ends of the earth?"

Grace frowned. "The earth doesn't really have ends."

"It does not," Dad said. "But at one time, people didn't know the earth was round, like a globe. They thought it was flat. The ends of the earth would be the edge of the flat disk. Although, as I recall, the ancient Greeks figured out the earth was round. But maybe not until after that myth came about. Or maybe it was only a metaphor – a figure of speech, not meant to be taken as real."

They went down into the ancient city. It was perched among the mountains, with green valleys beyond the ruined town. Other tourists wandered among the ruins, walking on gray stone pavement. In many places, the only parts of the ruined buildings remaining were low walls. It looked strange to see people in bright clothing, holding cameras, among the faded city.

"People lived here over three thousand years ago," Dad said. "It would have been a small town in the beginning. There's a story that a dragon, Python, guarded these hills. Then the god Apollo killed Python so Delphi became his. The people started worshiping Apollo, and the city grew."

They paused by a small stone building. The front was open except for two columns. Dad said, "Some of these temples are from the fourth and fifth century BCE, about 2,500 years ago. Apollo had different forms, and one of them was a dolphin. They worshiped his dolphin form here. That's how the city got its name. Delphi means dolphin. Thousands of tourists visited in ancient times. People came to ask the Oracle for advice."

"What's an Oracle? Some kind of fish?" Jaden chuckled. "Get it? Dolphin god, fish?"

Dad ruffled his hair. "The Oracle was a prophet. It was always a woman, a priestess. When someone asked for advice, the Oracle would enter into a trance. Then she gave an answer, which a priest explained. People would ask for advice on everything from whom to marry to whether they should go to war."

"How did she know what to say?" Grace asked. "She couldn't have really known the future. But people wouldn't keep coming if she was wrong, would they?"

"She didn't have to be right, she just had to be vague," Dad said. "She would give answers that could mean anything. One king asked for advice before going to war. The Oracle told him that if he went to war, a great empire would fall. He thought she meant his enemy would fall. But it was the king's empire that fell. She would have been right no matter who won. Or she might give advice that was always good. Say you read a horoscope in the newspaper. It says, 'Today is a good day to spend time with family.' How could that be wrong?"

Grace smiled and took her dad's hand. "So were the Oracles faking?"

"Maybe, but more likely they believed in what they did. Belief is powerful. It's probably another reason a lot of prophecies turned true. If someone promises a leader he's going to win a battle, he keeps fighting even when things look bad. He's more likely to win if he doesn't give up."

Dad boosted Jaden onto the platform in front of the small stone building. Then he helped Grace up. "If we decide we're going have fun on this vacation, we'll have more fun. But if you decide you don't want to be here, you'll look for things to complain about. That would ruin the fun."

"That would be silly." Grace did miss her friends back home, but this was still the best summer ever. She looked at the building in front of them. One of the columns had a piece in the middle that was different, as if it had been broken and repaired. "How did this building last when everything else fell down?"

"This has been rebuilt," Dad said. "Archaeologists

excavated the site. Most of it was probably covered with dirt and grass. They dug down, marking everything they found. Then they cleaned up the site and put some of the buildings back together. The rebuilt structures give an idea of how the city looked in ancient times. See how parts of the columns are white, and that section is darker gray? The white is the original marble, a type of stone. Where parts of the columns were broken or stolen, they filled in the gaps with new material."

Jaden stared up at the column, which was as big around as he was and twice his height. "Why would somebody steal one of those?"

"Museums took things to put on display. Rich travelers took pieces back to show in their homes. Delphi was filled with statues in ancient times, but they've all been moved other places."

Jaden laughed. "Let's get a column for our living room!"

"We could take this whole temple and put it in the backyard," Grace said, smiling.

Dad chuckled. "We'd have the fanciest garden shed in the neighborhood!"

He led the way past other ruined buildings. "Theft

can still be a problem, but now laws protect sites like this. Two hundred years ago, taking a statue or a piece of old building wasn't considered stealing. People thought it was okay to go to another country and take old artifacts. A lot of treasures from Greece are in museums in the US and other places. Some people think everything should go back where it came from. Others think it's good that people can see great works of art and pieces of history without traveling too far."

Grace thought about that. It was amazing seeing things in person like this. But most people couldn't do that. Did they deserve a chance to see things in a museum? But who actually owned pieces of a city that had been abandoned centuries before?

Next they visited a gymnasium. In ancient times, a gymnasium was a school as well as a place for sports. Then they went to the Delphi stadium. It had gray stone benches in a long oval. They had been rebuilt on one side and rose up in row after row, like bleachers at a sports stadium. On the opposite side of the grassy open space, only a row of chunky rocks remained. Beyond them, the ground sloped steeply down to a walking path.

They had a snack and some water. Dad leafed through the guidebook. "They held the Pythian Games here every four years. Kind of like the Olympics. At first the games were music and poetry competitions, because Apollo was the god of music and the arts. Then they added athletic competitions. There was a big chariot race. Can you imagine it? These stands filled with crowds. Small chariots, only large enough for one man to stand up in, each pulled by four horses. Imagine the sounds of the horses' hooves pounding in the dirt, and the crowds cheering."

Grace tried to picture the stadium filled with ancient Greeks. Jaden ran down to the stadium floor and raced down it, pretending to drive a chariot. He wasn't exactly a roaring crowd, but he was loud. A nearby man muttered something about noisy kids.

Dad groaned. "How does Jaden still have energy after our hike? We'd better catch him."

They walked down the long stadium, expecting to see Jaden on his way back after making the turn at the far end. But they didn't see him, and even his shouts had vanished. Dad looked worried. Grace said, "I'll bet he's hiding again, to trick us."

"You're probably right. That has to stop. It's too dangerous if we don't know where he is."

Where would Jaden hide? He must be behind one of the walls or boulders, or in the bushes at the edge of the stadium.

Grace spotted some yellow tape and wooden boards blocking off one section. A sign had a message in several languages. The English said, "Danger – Falling Rocks."

She grabbed her father's sleeve. "Dad? You don't suppose Jaden went there, do you?"

Chapter Three

LOST AND FOUND

Dad looked at the sign, the barrier, and the rocky slope behind it. "Wait here." Dad climbed up the stadium seats, heading for the dangerous area. Grace's breath caught in her chest, while her mind whirled. Jaden often got into mischief, and he wasn't afraid of much. But would he really have gone someplace so clearly out of bounds? He usually followed the rules, so long as the rules were very, very clear. The barrier and the sign in English were clear. He couldn't pretend he didn't understand.

"Wait, Dad!" Grace called. "Maybe he didn't go that way."

Dad hesitated, about to duck under the tape. "I can't take that chance."

If Jaden was hiding, what would persuade him to come out? Grace turned around, scanning the area. "Jaden! You got us again. Come out now before Dad gets in trouble."

They waited, listening. All of Grace's senses were alert. Colors seemed extra bright in the slanting late-afternoon sun. A breeze brushed past her face, bringing a spicy scent from the nearby bushes. Voices murmured in the distance, other tourists exploring the ruins.

Something crashed through the trees. A fist-sized rock bounced down the slope toward the bleachers. It hit a stony patch and split in two. A chunk flew toward Dad, landing a foot away. A small brown goat darted out of the trees and headed downhill. No Jaden followed.

Grace searched for signs of her brother. Several short, square columns stood in a line at this end of the stadium. Each was large enough to hide a young boy. She ran toward them and darted between two, whipping her head left and right. No sign of Jaden.

But what was that sound? She heard people speaking in a foreign language, but among them, a familiar voice. Grace ran a few more steps, until she could see down to the walking path below the stadium. "Dad, here he is!"

Jaden looked up and pointed as their father joined Grace. The group around Jaden waved and turned away.

"Wait there," Dad called out. He led Grace down by an easier path. "What was that about?"

Jaden shrugged. "They thought I was lost. I tried to explain that you were right there, but they didn't understand English."

Dad put his hands on his hips. "Jaden, how many times have I told you to stay within sight?"

Jaden thought a minute. "About a billion?"

Dad sighed and shook his head. "And I'm telling you again. You scared us."

Jaden looked surprised. "I didn't go far. I saw an animal in the bushes, and I thought it was a dog, and maybe it was hurt or trapped. But it was a goat and it ran off."

"You shouldn't approach strange animals. I know most animals treat you like a long-lost brother, but a dog could bite. Anyway, we didn't know where you were. That was scary."

"Oh. I'm sorry." Jaden took Dad's hand and was quiet as they left the ruins. Grace gave him a sympathetic look. He could never resist animals.

It was one thing they had in common, when they were so different in most ways.

They stopped for dinner at a small restaurant. They all shared a Greek salad, which had pieces of tomato, cucumber, bell pepper and red onion. It also had black olives and chunks of salty feta cheese. Grace traded the olives she didn't like for the cucumbers Jaden didn't like. Next came gyros, sandwiches of grilled meat on pita bread. The round, flat pita bread was fresh and warm. The juicy chicken had a lemony taste and a yogurt sauce.

They spent the night at a campground near Delphi. The campground had a little store, a fancy restaurant, a playground, a swimming pool, and even an Internet café. Grace and Jaden swam, while Dad wrote notes for his articles.

In the morning, they took a taxi to a nearby small town on the coast. Around the city, mountains sloped down to the edge of the water. The family stood on the dock and looked across the bay. The blue sky arched overhead, and the deeper blue water glinted in the sunlight. Across the bay, the long chain of mountains made a softer purplish-blue line in between sky and water.

Someone called out to them and Dad turned to wave. "There's our boat pilot and guide. For the next few days, we'll be living on a boat, sailing the Greek islands, and swimming at remote beaches!"

A little shiver of excitement ran through Grace. She had never been on a boat before. Would she like it? Would it be scary? Would she get seasick?

Grace liked swimming in the pool. She wasn't so sure about swimming in the ocean. They'd swum in a lake once back home. The water was dark and murky, so you couldn't see anything below the surface. A fish had brushed past her and she'd screamed. Jaden teased her, and even Dad had chuckled once he was sure Grace wasn't hurt. She hadn't gone back into the lake after that. The ocean would be even worse, because it had waves and big animals. What if she met a shark or octopus?

She hoped the trip would be fun. Too bad she couldn't tell the future. But maybe Dad was right. If she decided to have a good time, she would.

Chapter Four

WHAT ABOUT MONSTERS?

The man shook hands with Dad. "I'm Nikos Papadopoulos, your skipper." He was short and muscular, with short dark hair. He shook hands with the children too. "You can call me Nikos or Skipper."

Jaden studied him. "Do you skip a lot?"

Nikos chuckled. "The skipper is the captain of a boat or ship. Let me show you where you'll be spending the next few days." He led them to a small boat moored nearby. It was white, with two triangular sails on a tall mast. "This is the Wave Dancer," he said proudly.

Nikos helped them onto the deck. A woman with a dark ponytail greeted them. "This is Daphne," Nikos said. "She's a biologist and also our deckhand."

The woman smiled. "That means I help out

with all the jobs needed to keep the boat running smoothly."

"And you're a scientist who studies living things," Dad said. "Do you have a specialty in biology?"

"I study the native animals in the Greek islands." Daphne turned to the kids. "On this trip, I hope you'll help me. We'll count some of the animals and birds we see."

Jaden's grin split his face. He and Grace nodded. Studying animals sounded like fun!

Nikos led the way down below, inside the boat. A wooden table stood between blue bench couches. Everything was attached to the floor so it couldn't slide. One wall held a kitchenette, with stove, sink, counter space and cupboards.

"There are four cabins," Nikos said. "Two for you and two for the crew. We have two showers and toilets down here, plus a shower on deck, for cleaning off after a swim. Stow your bags and we'll set sail. Everything has to be put away properly, so it's secure when the boat rocks."

They put their things in lockers and cabinets. Grace crawled onto her bed, a mattress on a

platform, and looked out the tiny window. The
sea's surface was just below. They would be living,
even sleeping, right out on the water!

She hurried after the others back up to the deck.
Another woman boarded the boat. She carried
several cloth bags, the kind you can reuse at the
grocery store. "Last-minute supplies!" she said
cheerfully.

"Eleni is our cook," Nikos said. "She is also an
environmental researcher."

"That means she helps me study the animals," Daphne explained.

Eleni had big sunglasses, a big smile, and dark reddish hair held back by a purple headband. "I hope we'll see some dolphins on this trip. I love them."

"Me too!" Jaden said. Grace nodded. This was going to be a great trip!

Nikos said, "Okay, children, put your life jackets on so we can sail! You need to wear life jackets whenever you're on deck. You can take them off below."

Dad helped them put on the orange lifejackets that would keep them afloat if they fell in the water. Grace hoped they wouldn't need them. Swimming in the ocean would be bad enough without falling in by accident!

Eleni went below to stow the groceries. Nikos and Daphne untied the boat and adjusted the sails. They headed away from the dock. The wind blew Grace's hair into her face. She pulled her hair into a ponytail and put on sunglasses, because the sun reflecting off the water was so bright. They had used sunscreen before leaving the campground.

The boat bumped over waves, making it hard to balance. Grace sat on deck and watched the scenery. The sky and the water were so blue. They sailed past little villages on shore. White houses shone in the sunlight. A man on a donkey moving slowly along a rocky cliff.

They passed other boats, from tiny fishing boats to large, fancy cruising ships. Sometimes birds flew overhead. Eleni put out meze, appetizers. One plate held triangles of pita bread. A bowl had a pale, creamy dip in it. Nikos and Daphne scooped up dip with pieces of pita bread.

Grace was hungry, so she did the same. The dip was interesting, kind of salty. "What is it?"

"Taramosalata," Nikos said. "One of our favorite dishes in Greece. It's carp roe, blended with bread, onion, little lemon juice and olive oil."

Grace frowned. "Carp roe? What's that?"

"Carp is a kind of fish. Roe is the eggs."

Grace wrinkled her nose and put down her half-eaten piece of bread. "We're eating fish eggs?"

The grown-ups laughed. "You seemed to like it until you knew what it was," Dad commented.

Jaden stuffed a piece of bread piled with dip into

his mouth. "Mmm, fish eggs!" he mumbled around the food. Grace knew he was just showing off. Still, she forced herself to finish the piece she'd taken. Chicken eggs were all right, and fish was all right, but somehow fish eggs didn't seem like food. At least she had other choices: salad, meatballs, and grape leaves stuffed with rice.

After lunch, Grace noticed a dark shape in the water ahead. She stood and leaned over the railing to get a better view.

"Aargh!" Hands grabbed her from behind.

Grace jumped and grabbed onto the railing tighter. "Jaden!"

He laughed. "What are you looking at?"

"See that dark spot?" It was 20 or 30 feet off to the side now.

Jaden nodded. "Sea monster."

"It is not!"

"How do you know, if you've never seen one?"

Grace rolled her eyes. "I know because sea monsters don't exist."

"You can't prove that."

Grace sighed and turned to the woman standing nearby. "Eleni, do you believe in sea monsters?"

"Well, I've never seen one," Eleni said. "The ancient Greeks had a lot of legends about monsters though. Many of them caused trouble for sailors. Scylla and Charybdis lived on either side of a narrow channel of water. Three times a day, Charybdis gulped down huge amounts of seawater. This caused whirlpools, where the water swirled around and sucked down boats. But if sailors tried to avoid Charybdis, they might get too close to Scylla. She had six heads on long, snakelike necks. Each head had three rows of sharp teeth. She devoured anyone who got too close. In the story of Odysseus, Scylla ate six of his sailors."

"There, see!" Jaden told Grace. "I told you monsters were real."

Eleni chuckled. "I wouldn't go that far. These are legends, stories that may or may not have some truth to them. Greek myths are a lot of fun, but that doesn't mean the stories are true."

"But they could be," Jaden said.

Eleni shrugged. "More likely they were warnings. Sailors sometimes disappeared at sea. Maybe the boat sank in a storm, or pirates attacked. The stories acted as a warning: Be careful out there!"

Grace looked nervously at the water. "Sailing isn't that dangerous now, is it?"

"You always have to be careful on the ocean," Eleni said. "But this boat is strong. And we won't be going far from land. If we get bad weather, we'll go someplace safe." She tapped Grace's orange life jacket. "And if there is an accident, you have these."

That was only sort of comforting. Life jacket or no life jacket, Grace did not want to fall overboard.

Eleni put an arm around Grace's shoulders. "Don't worry. Nikos, Daphne and I spend most of our time sailing this boat. We've never had a major accident or lost a passenger. Or seen a sea monster."

"What about sharks?" Grace asked.

"There are sharks in the area, but most types are harmless. We won't be swimming any place where sharks have attacked people. You know, sharks aren't monsters. They are simply animals doing what nature tells them to do. They're not evil or mean."

"I guess. But I still only want to see one in at the aquarium."

"I understand," Eleni said. "But you know, people have killed far more sharks, than sharks have killed people."

Grace was scared of sharks, but she didn't want them dead. All wild animals deserved a good life. She had more questions, but the boat was nearing land.

"Next stop, the Underworld!" Nikos called out.

Chapter Five

GOING UNDER

Grace glanced at Eleni. "The Underworld? What does he mean?"

She looked mysterious. "You'll enjoy this."

Nikos called out to someone. Grace rushed to the railing and saw a blue flat-bottomed boat, with a man paddling it. "You'll visit the cave this way," Nikos said. "Our boat is too big."

A rounded cave opened in the cliff ahead. The ocean water went right into the cave, with room for a small boat to float through. They would be going underground. Maybe that's what Nikos meant by the Underworld.

Daphne got into the smaller boat. Dad helped Jaden and Grace down to her. Grace sat on the front bench next to Daphne. Dad and Jaden sat behind them. The boat pilot, seated at the back, steered into the cave opening. The boat bobbed gently as the man controlled it with slow paddle strokes.

At first Grace couldn't see anything in the dim light. She was still wearing sunglasses. She took them off and tucked them in her shorts pocket.

As they got farther from the bright opening, the pilot turned on a spotlight. It picked out an amazing sight above them. Tiny stalactites, thinner than pencils, glowed golden and shiny with drips of water. They were packed close together, too many to count.

"Some of these formations were formed thousands of years ago," Daphne said. "The water level was lower then. That's why you have stalagmites under the water."

"Some stalactites are still being formed now, right?" Dad asked.

"Yes, you can see the drops of water at work. It takes hundreds of thousands of years to create these formations."

Some columns jutted up from beneath the water. The ceiling reflected on the water, making rippling mirror images. It was hard to tell the difference between the reflections and the real columns.

Around the edges of the water, stalactites from the ceiling met up with stalagmites from the ground. Columns of all shapes and sizes glistened wetly.

"We're at the very tip of mainland Greece," Daphne said. This area is called Cape Matapan or Cape Tainaron. This was an important place in ancient times. The early Greeks believed that a cave was the entrance to Hades. That's the Underworld, land of the dead. Some people think this very cave was the entrance."

"How far does the cave go?" Dad asked.

"There are several miles of passages," Daphne said. "But not enough to reach Hades! The stories say several Greek heroes went down to the Underworld through a cave."

A drop of water landed on Grace's nose. She jumped and brushed it off. It was cold compared to the comfortable temperature of the cave. Another drop landed in her hair.

"One of those heroes was Orpheus." Daphne's soft voice echoed spookily. "Orpheus's wife, Eurydice, died right after their wedding. She was bitten by a snake. Orpheus was so upset, he decided to go down to the world of death. That was very dangerous, of course. But Orpheus had a special gift, the gift of music. Some stories say his father was Apollo, god of the arts. Orpheus played the lyre, a stringed instrument like a guitar. In Hades, he played the lyre and sang, begging the dead to give him back his wife. What do you think happened?"

Grace was about to answer when Jaden said, "They killed him!"

Daphne glanced back and shook her head. "You underestimate the power of music. They agreed to give back Eurydice. However, there was one condition he had to follow. She had to walk behind him, and he could not look back."

"That doesn't sound so hard," Grace said.

Daphne smiled. "They climbed the path through the darkness. Orpheus knew Eurydice should be right behind him. Still, he wanted to make sure. He resisted the urge to look back, knowing he would lose her. Finally he reached daylight. In his relief, he turned to her, but it was too soon. She was still in the cavern. The moment he saw her, she whispered, 'Farewell,' and disappeared."

"That's sad," Grace said. "Couldn't he go back and get her again?"

Daphne shook her head. "The gods would not allow him to enter Hades a second time while he was alive. He wandered alone, playing his lyre, until he died."

Dad said, "There's a moral to that story, but I'm not sure what it is."

"Maybe not to give up too soon," Daphne said. "If you're doing something difficult, you have to do it all the way. Don't stop short of the finish line and celebrate too early."

"He only had to wait a few more seconds," Grace said. "How hard can it be, to not look back? And his poor wife had to stay in the Underworld because of him."

"It might be harder than you think," Dad said.

Jaden poked Grace in the back. "I'll bet you can't go through this whole cave without looking back here."

"I could too!" Grace said. "But I don't want to miss anything."

"Bet you can't," Jaden said. "Try it. You can look to the left and right, but not behind you."

"Fine." Grace had plenty to see in front and to the sides. Why would she want to look back at her brother anyway? She saw him often enough.

They drifted, silent except for the dripping water

and the soft splash of the boatman's paddle. It was like floating through a magical fairyland castle. Grace never wanted to leave.

A spooky sound whispered through the cave, a low humming. The back of Grace's neck pickled. She sat up straighter, forcing herself to keep facing forward. "I know that's you, Jaden."

He chuckled behind her.

"Would you like a more cheerful story about the Underworld?" Daphne asked. "One of the great Greek heroes was Hercules. He had to do twelve labors, or difficult chores. The final one was the most dangerous. Hercules had to go down to the underworld and kidnap Cerberus. Cerberus was like a giant dog with three heads and a dragon's tail. He guarded the entrance to Hades and kept the living from entering."

"Cerberus sounds cool," Jaden said. "A dog with three heads and a dragon's tail! I want one."

Dad chuckled. "You find an animal shelter with a dog like that, and it's yours."

"So Hercules went into the cave and down to the underworld," Daphne said. "He had to get past many ghosts and monsters. Finally Hercules found Cerberus and wrestled him. Hercules captured the beast and brought him out of the underworld. This fulfilled his twelfth task. He then let Cerberus go back to Hades to continue his work as a guard. Hercules became Greece's greatest hero."

"For wrestling a poor dog?" Jaden said. "Big deal."

"Was Cerberus a monster?" Grace asked.

"Hmm, interesting question," Daphne said. "What makes something a monster? Cerberus was scary, but he was doing his job. And it was an important job, keeping living people out of the land of the dead."

"Hey, can we pause for a minute?" Dad asked. "I want to take some pictures." Again Grace had to resist the urge to glance back. It was harder than she'd expected. She didn't need to see her father, but it was instinct to look at someone when they talked.

The pilot let the boat drift gently. Dad's camera flash lit up the area every 30 seconds or so. Spots filled Grace's vision in the darkness afterward.

Cold water dripped on Grace's neck. She squirmed and brushed it away. Another splash of water came, this one bigger. Grace glanced up at the ceiling. Was she right under a wet spot? Dad's camera flashed, blinding her again. Before her eyes could adjust, more cold water dripped on her head.

"Jaden!" she snapped, without turning. "I know that's you. That's not fair."

He laughed. Dad said, "I didn't see what you did, Jaden, but stop it."

Grace grumbled, "Orpheus was lucky he didn't have a brother."

Dad finished taking his pictures and the pilot rowed them forward again. They headed for a narrow space between two columns. "I can touch the ceiling!" Jaden exclaimed. The boat rocked suddenly. Grace gasped and grabbed Daphne's arm.

"No you don't," Dad said. His words were followed by a thump, and the boat settled down. Grace guessed Jaden had tried to stand up. And still she had not looked back. So there!

The boat turned back toward the entrance. Grace tried to take in everything she could see. She never wanted to forget this.

They drifted through the cave opening. Grace blinked against the bright outside light. She couldn't see anything. Oh right, her sunglasses. She fumbled for them.

The boat turned suddenly to the right, throwing

Grace toward the outside edge. A second later, something bumped against her back. Jaden called out, "Ahoy, Wind Dancer!" The boat rocked. Blinded and off-balance, Grace flailed her arms, trying to grab onto anything. Her elbow hit Jaden in the stomach. He grunted and fell forward on top of her.

Grace slid off the bench, her arms and legs tangling with each other and Jaden. Water splashed over her face. Were they falling overboard? She opened her mouth to scream.

Chapter Six

DANGERS ON LAND AND SEA

Hands grabbed her. The rocking slowed. Jaden had a knee in her stomach until someone pulled him off. Daphne helped Grace back onto the bench. "This is why we use a flat-bottomed boat, instead of a narrow canoe. The wide boat is more stable." She turned to give Jaden a stern look. "You could have tipped the boat over otherwise."

"And if you'd fallen in and gotten your boots wet, we wouldn't be able to take our hike," Dad said. "You would have ruined the afternoon for everyone."

Jaden gave a sheepish grin. "Sorry."

Grace was still trembling from the fright. But she was fine, safe inside the small boat. Even if she had fallen in the water, she had her life vest on. But the thought of falling overboard made her feel sick. She tried to think of something else. "And I did not look back once!" she snapped at Jaden. "Not until we were both out in the sunshine."

"Yeah, you did good." He grinned. "You won, so you can have my fish egg paste tonight."

Grace stuck out her tongue. Dad said, "She can have your dessert tonight." Jaden made a face and sighed.

The boat pilot took them to shore. Daphne hopped out and held the boat while the others got out. They took off their life vests and left them in the boat.

"We'll take a walk and meet up with our boat later," Daphne said.

A small lighthouse stood on the very tip of the land. They climbed the rocky slope near it and looked out over the water, catching their breath. The fresh breeze cooled them after the hike. The ocean seemed to go on forever. The sight made Grace feel funny. So much water! They were sailing across that on a little boat. Who knew what dangers were out there?

They walked across a hilltop for about half an hour. The ground was rocky, with short, yellow weeds. Most of the color came from the blue sky and the ocean beyond the rocky coast. In the distance, a cluster of stone houses and tall square towers rose up. It looked like something out of a movie.

"The stone towers are traditional in this area," Daphne said. "People lived in family groups, or clans, each led by a chief. The clans often fought with each other. They built the towers as protection, against both foreigners and other clans. The last big feud happened in 1870. The Army had to come in to make peace."

She gazed up at the stone towers and sighed. "A lot of the towers are empty now. Many people moved away in the past century or so."

"Why?" Dad asked.

"The area isn't great for farming," Daphne said. "People went to bigger cities to find work. Some moved to the United States or other countries. Now there are some fishing villages, and tourism, but little else."

Maybe that's why the area seemed so lonely. It was sad that people had to leave their hometowns to find work. But maybe some people preferred big cities.

They reached a mound of stones. An arched doorway showed that the pile was once a building. It had partly collapsed.

"There used to be several temples to the Greek gods along here," Daphne said. "This one was Poseidon's

Sanctuary. Poseidon was the sea god. Later the temple became a Christian church. A lot of the ancient Greek temples were turned into Christian churches once Christianity became common. Some of them are still used today."

They walked on until they reached a statue of a man riding a dolphin. "This is the poet Arion," Daphne said. "He was traveling from Italy to Greece when he was kidnapped by pirates. He jumped off the ship to escape. Arion prayed to Apollo, and the god sent dolphins to help. They carried the poet here to safety. At least, that's the story."

Riding a dolphin sounded so cool! It would almost be worth falling off a boat if you could be rescued that way. Maybe. But riding a dolphin without falling overboard would be even better.

They walked onward. Something rustled in the grass nearby. Grace paused to look. Maybe it was a bird or a small animal such as a rabbit. She wasn't sure what animals they had in Greece.

Jaden stopped beside her. "What are you looking at?"

"Some kind of animal, I think."

The grasses rustled again. A long snake slithered past them, a few feet away. It was three feet long, pale with dark spots. Grace backed up. Snakes could be dangerous.

"Cool!" Jaden took a step toward it.

Grace grabbed his arm. "Wait!" Dad pulled Jaden and Grace farther away. Daphne looked down at the snake from a few feet away. "That's a Balkan Whip Snake. They're not venomous – no poison – but they can bite. In any case, leave it alone so you don't hurt the snake."

"But I've seen guys on TV pick up snakes," Jaden said.

Daphne frowned. "Some experts know how to handle snakes. They still risk injuring the snake, though. It's best to leave wild animals alone."

"Especially if you don't know about the animal," Dad said. "Some snakes are poisonous. Remember, one killed Eurydice, Orpheus's wife."

"But I like snakes," Jaden said.

"I do too," Daphne said. "Snakes do a lot of good. They eat insects and rodents such as rats. Rodents can eat people's food and carry disease. Without snakes, we might have far too many mice and rats. Snakes are part of nature's balance. We should leave them alone – for their sake and ours!"

Jaden sighed and they kept walking. "Do you know the story of Medusa?" Daphne asked. "She had snakes instead of hair. Anyone who looked at her face was turned to stone. The hero Perseus finally killed her. He used a mirrored shield so he wouldn't have to look directly at her. When he cut off her head, the winged horse Pegasus was born from her blood."

"A horse with wings would be the best pet ever," Jaden said.

Grace could agree with that. "Aren't there any Greek girl heroes?"

"Absolutely," Daphne said. "In fact, the goddess Athena gave the mirrored shield to Perseus. Without her help, he wouldn't have defeated Medusa. Artemis, the twin sister of Apollo, was another great goddess. She was goddess of the hunt and she protected young women. She also helped women giving birth."

They headed down a rocky path toward a village on the coast. The waters of the bay made a beautiful curve, meeting white beaches. The town nestled between hills and the water. As they approached, Daphne told them about several other goddesses. Then she said, "Not every famous female in ancient Greece was a goddess. There were mortal heroines as well, ordinary people rather than goddesses. One of them was called Atalanta. She was abandoned and raised by a wild bear. She became a very famous hunter."

They entered the town, only a few dozen buildings. "About thirty people live here," Daphne said. "During the summer, there are probably more tourists here than locals."

They went to a restaurant and sat on a patio, looking out over the water. The setting sun turned the sky pink. Grace had a tasty seafood pasta.

Then they went down to the dock to board the boat. Nikos played guitar and sang Greek songs. Stars filled the dark sky above. It had been a long day, and Grace was falling asleep when Dad sent her off to bed. The boat rocked gently. It was comforting, and Grace drifted off to sleep.

She woke in the middle of the night. The boat was rocking much more. Waves crashed against the side of the boat, and the wood creaked as if it wanted to split apart. Voices came from the deck above, but she couldn't hear what they were saying. Did they sound worried? Scared?

Grace crept out of bed and made her way through the kitchen. She grabbed onto the furniture for balance as the boat tossed her one way and then the other. She had to cling tightly to the railing as she went up the ladder. All the grown-ups were on deck.

Dad glanced her way and hurried over. "It's all right, just a storm. We're going to move someplace safer."

Why did they need to go someplace safer if everything was all right? Grace shivered and tried to shake the hair out of her eyes.

"Let's get you into a life vest." Dad ushered Grace back below and got a life vest for her. Grace was still shivering. It was hard to believe it had been so hot that afternoon. Now with the wind whistling down the open hatch, her bare feet felt like blocks of ice.

Dad wrapped a blanket around her, and Grace curled up in the corner of the couch. Jaden stumbled out and Dad got him a life vest and blanket. "You two stay down here," Dad said. "I'm going back up to see if I can help."

"Put a life vest on first!" Grace insisted.

Dad smiled. "Of course, you're right." He found an adult life vest and snapped it on. Grace felt a little better. She didn't think anyone would be able to swim with the sea so rough. But at least a life vest would keep them afloat if someone fell overboard.

Grace and Jaden huddled together. The boat rocked and shuddered. Grace's head hurt and she felt queasy. She tried to take deep, slow breaths so she wouldn't be sick. Jaden dozed off against her shoulder, but she couldn't sleep. She watched the clock on the wall as the minutes slowly ticked by. An hour passed, then another. Would this night ever end?

Chapter Seven

ANCiENT DiSASTERS

Finally the horrible rocking slowed. The boat bobbed gently again. The wind no longer roared, and laughter came from the deck above. Grace slowly uncurled her stiff body. She slipped out from behind the table and staggered the few feet to the kitchen counter. Her legs wobbled and she felt clumsy.

Dad and the crew came down and headed to their cabins to put on dry clothes. Grace got out mugs and hot chocolate mix. Eleni was the first one back. "Great idea," she said. "I'll heat up the milk."

Dad came in and stroked Grace's hair. "You OK, kiddo?"

She nodded. The sick feeling was leaving her stomach, to be replaced by hunger. "Where are we now?"

"We're in a bay, protected from the wind. It will be a nice place to swim tomorrow."

Grace didn't want to go in the ocean. Not after it had showed how rough it could be.

In the morning, Grace went on deck with her life jacket on. They were tied up at a dock at the edge of a town. The town was tucked in the curve of a bay surrounded by land on three sides. "This is the Greek island of Santorini," Daphne said.

Steep cliffs were white on top, as if covered by snow, but Daphne said it was white rock. She explained how a volcano shaped the island over the centuries. "This bay is actually the center of the ancient volcano. The volcano exploded, and then collapsed where the explosion happened. Ash from the explosion traveled for miles. It buried an ancient city on Santorini under layers of ash. The people escaped, but the deep ash preserved the wall paintings and objects left behind. Archeologists are excavating the site."

Grace looked at the boats bobbing in the water, and the white buildings clustered at the bottom of the cliffs. "Could that happen again?"

"Yes, someday," Daphne said. "The last volcano

eruption here was in 1950, but it was small. Greece has earthquakes all the time, but most of them aren't serious. Maybe you feel a little shaking, but nothing is damaged. The last really serious earthquake was in 1999. It destroyed many buildings in Athens and left a lot of people homeless."

Maybe land wasn't safer than the ocean after all! But the people in the town were cheerful and friendly. They waved and greeted the group as they explored and did some shopping. No one seemed worried about earthquakes or volcanoes.

Eleni served lunch on the boat, Greek salad and tyropita, flaky pastry layered with mild white cheese. Then they went swimming from the beach. Grace kept her life jacket on, even though Dad said she didn't have to there, and stayed near shore. Splashing in the shallow water was fun, but she got nervous if she went too deep.

That evening, Eleni taught Dad how to make Greek-style grilled fish and roasted potatoes with lemon juice. They watched a beautiful sunset, the sky turning red. Then they lay on the deck and looked up at the stars. Nikos told Greek stories about the stars. Some of the groups of stars were supposed to be Greek heroes in the sky.

In the morning, they had Greek yogurt with peaches and honey, plus bread and jam. Then they sailed to a large island called Crete. They docked at the island's capital city, Heraklion. Their boat pulled along the docks among many other sailboats and speedboats. Tall buildings rose up beyond the docks. An airplane flew low overhead. Grace, Jaden, and their father followed Daphne along the docks. Nikos stayed with the boat, and Eleni went grocery shopping.

Daphne waved for a taxi and gave the driver instructions in Greek. Then she turned to address Grace's family in the back seat. "Crete is the birthplace of Europe's first advanced civilization. They were called the Minoans. They first came here over four thousand years ago. They built huge palaces in several cities.

An earthquake destroyed everything around 1700 BC. I told you Greece has a lot of earthquake activity, but this one was huge. What do you think the people did after that disaster?"

"They all died," Jaden suggested.

Grace knew that couldn't be right. They wouldn't have done anything after the disaster if they'd all died. "Did they move someplace safer?" That's what she would do.

Daphne shook her head. "The Minoans stayed. They built even bigger and better palaces."

"Why wouldn't they go someplace safe?"

"Maybe they didn't know where to go that would be safe," Daphne suggested.

"Most places have some danger," Dad said. "In America, we have earthquakes in California. Tornadoes on the Great Plains. Severe winter storms in the Northeast. Science can help us predict when disasters might happen, so we can prepare. We can make buildings that should survive earthquakes. We can take shelter when a tornado is predicted. We can buy supplies if a storm might knock out the heat and leave us stranded. We can be ready, but we can't avoid every problem."

"People also had other reasons for staying in one place," Daphne said. "Volcanic soil is very good for farming. The coast provides lots of fish. Steep cliffs offer protection from enemies. This was a great place, most of the time. Plus, for some people, staying and starting over is a way of fighting back. It shows you won't let anything stop you."

Grace considered. "I suppose if there was one safe place, everyone would want to live there. There wouldn't be enough space for everybody."

"Right," Daphne said. "Then people fight, and that's dangerous too! There are always trade-offs between good and bad. Anyway, the Minoans rebuilt. Their new palaces lasted about 250 years. The cities were destroyed again around 1450 BC."

"What happened then?" Jaden asked.

"The Minoans stayed around for a while, but they didn't rebuild their huge palaces. Other groups came and went. It became part of the Roman Empire. Then it was part of the Byzantine Empire, ruled by Christians. Arabs took over the island, and then the Byzantines took it back. It was even ruled by Venice, Italy, for a while. Then the Arabs again."

All this history was awfully complicated. "They must have been fighting all the time," Grace said. She glanced out the window as a motorbike squeezed past the taxi, honking its horn.

"Well, we are talking about thousands of years of history," Daphne said. "Crete only officially became part of Greece in 1913. I don't expect you to remember all of this. But it explains why there are so many different kinds of buildings. Christian churches, Muslim mosques, European palaces. You'll find them all here. But we're heading for one of the oldest parts. The Minoan palace of Knossos."

They left the main part of the city and drove down a winding road with trees on either side. A few minutes later, they pulled into a parking lot. "Welcome to Knossos," Daphne said. "An ancient palace of luxury and wonder."

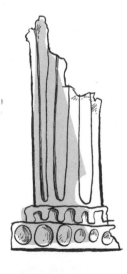

Chapter Eight

THE MINOTAUR

They wandered among the ruins. Some walls were only waist high, with rough gray stones showing. In other places, buildings had been rebuilt and had smooth walls and colorful paint. They went into different rooms, looking at wall paintings and giant clay jars. Grace's favorite place was the Queen's bedroom. A large painting of dolphins filled one wall.

"They even had plumbing here," Daphne said. "They built pipes to bring water in and out of the buildings. The first flush toilet was at Knossos thousands of years ago."

In another room, a colorful painting on the wall showed a large bull. Skinny young women with black hair stood on either side of it. A man was upside down on the bull's back. "This is a copy of a painting found here," Daphne said. "It shows a sport called bull leaping. When the bull charges, an acrobat grabs its horns. He or she does a somersault onto the bull's back. Then the person jumps off."

Dad said, "No, Jaden, you cannot try that."

They all laughed, but Jaden studied the painting as if memorizing it.

"Fortunately, there are no cattle on Crete today," Daphne said. "Jaden won't be able to find a bull or even a cow to leap!"

"Hey, speaking of bulls, isn't Crete where the Minotaur was supposed to be?" Dad asked.

Daphne nodded. "Legend says the Minotaur was half man and half bull. King Minos had a labyrinth built. A labyrinth is like a maze, with lots of passageways. It's easy to get lost in one. The myth says Minos sent the Minotaur into the labyrinth. Minos also sent in his enemies. They could never find their way out, and the Minotaur would eat them."

"Cool!" Jaden said.

"Poor Minotaur," Dad said. "Given nothing to eat but people."

Daphne led the way back out into the sunshine. "The king of Athens had to send seven young men and seven young women to Crete every year. They were given to the Minotaur as a sacrifice. Theseus, a prince from Athens, said he would go. Theseus wanted to kill the Minotaur and end the sacrifices. Theseus met Princess Ariadne, a daughter of King Minos. She fell in love with Theseus and wanted to help him, so she gave him a ball of thread. How do you think that helped?"

"Thread, like a piece of string?" Grace thought about it. She didn't see how you could kill a monster with a piece of string.

"She told him to tie one end at the entrance to the labyrinth," Daphne explained. "Then he should unravel the thread as he went through the passageways."

"I get it!" Grace said. "The thread would let him find his way back out."

"Exactly. He left a trail of thread behind him. Theseus killed the Minotaur and saved the other young people from Athens. With Ariadne's thread, he found his way out of the labyrinth."

"So she was a hero too," Grace said.

Daphne nodded. "She used her brains. Being smart is often more important than being tough."

They left the ruins and found a picnic spot near the road, in a grove of olive trees. Dad asked Daphne questions and took notes for his article. Jaden finished his sandwich first and said, "Let's play Theseus and the Minotaur. I get to be the Minotaur. I'll hide and you come find me."

Grace glanced at her father. He studied the landscape. Trees with thick, twisted trunks grew in rows as far as they could see. The ground underneath was grassy. "All right, but stay on this side of the road, and within shouting distance."

Grace swallowed her last bite of sandwich. "I want to be Ariadne, though, not Theseus. I'll go into the labyrinth myself."

"Fine." Jaden ran off among the trees.

Grace followed, pretending to unwind some string behind her. Since she didn't have a real ball of string, she kept checking where her father and Daphne were. Ahead of her, Jaden made grunting and snorting animal noises.

She lost sight of him for a minute. Grace looked back. She spotted a car passing on the road, but a tree blocked her view of Dad and Daphne. Best to make sure Jaden didn't go any farther.

Something rustled nearby. A low-hanging tree branch bounced and shook as if it had been pulled down. Grace ran around the tree. "Jaden –"

She stopped, staring at a long, bearded face with two big, curving horns. For a moment she thought she'd found the Minotaur!

The animal turned and bounced away. It was some kind of goat. Grace chuckled and continued her search for Jaden.

She rounded a tree and spotted him 20 feet away. He was sneaking up behind another of the goats. He had his hands out as if to grab it. That could not be a good idea! Jaden was taller than the goat, but the goat had horns over two feet long.

Before Grace could say or do anything, the goat looked back at Jaden. As soon as it saw him, it took off–horns lowered, heading directly for Grace!

Chapter Nine

CREATURES OF THE SEA

Grace spun around to run. But she couldn't outrun a goat!

A tree stood a few feet in front of her. She ran and jumped for the highest branch she could reach.

Her hands wrapped around the rough bark. Grace clung tightly and swung her legs as high as she could get them. Something brushed past her feet as she pulled them up.

The goat veered around the tree trunk and ran into the distance.

Grace let her feet hang down. They dangled a foot above the ground. She told her hands to let go, but they wouldn't listen. Her hands seem to think she was still in danger and needed to keep holding onto the tree branch.

Jaden ran up beside her. "That was cool! I wanted to jump over its back, like those acrobats in the bull painting. But it ran away. You did pretty good, even if you didn't do a flip."

Grace's arms trembled. She was going to drop out of the tree whether she wanted to or not.

Arms wrapped around her. "I've got you," Dad said as Grace's hand slipped. He lowered her gently to the ground. Grace leaned against him, glad she hadn't been knocked down and trampled. Dad said, "What was that all about? I heard someone yell."

Jaden explained about the goat leaping. "You said I wasn't allowed to try it with a bull, but you didn't say anything about a goat."

Dad sighed. "Jaden, you know you're not supposed to touch strange animals."

"Oh, right."

"It sound like you saw a Kri-Kri," Daphne said. "That's a local wild goat."

"The first one I saw, I thought for a second it was a Minotaur," Grace said.

They chuckled. "I doubt you'll find one of those," Daphne said. "It sounds like the most dangerous monster here is your brother. Come on back and have some baklava." Baklava was a sweet pastry with nuts and honey. Grace loved peeling apart the flaky layers.

"Let me guess," Jaden said. "I don't get any."

"Right," Dad said. "Maybe you are learning."

Back on the boat, the crew weighed anchor and headed out of the cove. "Let's see if we can find some dolphins!" Nikos said.

Grace and Jaden cheered. They sailed for a couple of hours without spotting any animals. Grace was half asleep by the time Daphne called out, "Dolphins off the starboard side!"

Grace sat up and looked around. She remembered that starboard and port were the sides of the boat, but which was which? Daphne was pointing over the right side of the boat. So right was starboard and left was port.

Grace joined Daphne at the rail. In the distance, a dozen sleek gray forms arched in the water. Nikos cut the engine and let the boat drift. The dolphins' curved backs rose just above the water, appearing and disappearing, over and over. With several dolphins in a row, it almost looked like one snakelike creature. Maybe that's how the story of sea monsters started.

Dad held up his camera. "Can't we get closer?"

"We don't want to disturb them," Nikos said. "If they're curious, they'll come to us."

One of the dolphins leapt, its whole body leaving the water before it crashed back down. Jaden cheered. A minute later, three dolphins leapt out of the water at the same time. Two more dolphins came close to the boat and seemed to be smiling up at the crew. Grace leaned over the rail, smiling back at them. Dad took pictures.

"Those are bottlenose dolphins," Daphne said. "They eat fish, shrimp, and squid. Sometimes they follow boats waiting for leftover scraps."

"Can we feed them?" Jaden asked.

Daphne shook her head. "We're not a fishing boat, so we don't have the right kind of scraps. I count eleven dolphins. How many do you count?"

Grace tried to count them. "It's hard because they keep moving, but I think eleven is right."

Jaden agreed, and Daphne made a note in a notebook. "I'm also noting exactly where we found them. Keeping track of information like this helps us know what's happening with the wildlife in and around Greece. Are the populations healthy? Are there any signs of danger? If there's a problem, we might catch it before it gets too bad."

"I want to swim with them," Jaden said. "Maybe they'll give me a ride, like that statute guy."

"That was just a story," Daphne said. "And we don't try to swim with the dolphins. People think dolphins are friendly because they look like they're smiling. But dolphins are wild animals, and they can be dangerous."

Dad asked, "Aren't there true stories of dolphins protecting swimmers from sharks?"

"Well, yes," Daphne said. "But it's hard to say if they really mean to protect people, or if they're just curious about the swimmers. Some companies arrange for tourists to swim with dolphins. People have been injured. Dolphins are big, heavy animals, and even if one is playing, it could break your bones.

"It's also not nice to the dolphins," Eleni added. "Wild dolphins are captured for those swimming experiences. How would you like to be penned up and forced to swim with people all day?"

Grace wouldn't like that at all. She stared down at the dolphins in the water. They were so beautiful, she understood why people wanted to swim with them. It sounded wonderful. But not if it was mean to the dolphins. At least she got to see them up close. And it was nice that people like Daphne were trying to help the dolphins. Maybe someday Grace would be able to work with dolphins and help them. That would be even better than riding one.

The dolphins played for a while before swimming away. Nikos turned the boat toward an island. The shore curved around them, making a small cove of water. Nikos called out from where he stood by the wheel, steering the boat. "We're going to anchor for a bit. Prepare for a swim!"

"And watch out for sea monsters!" Jaden hissed at Grace.

She didn't bother to tell him there were no sea monsters. Anyway, she was more worried about real animals, such as sharks. And even dolphins could be dangerous! She would stay close to land.

As soon as the boat stopped moving, the wind died down. Suddenly it was hot. Nikos said it was close to 100 degrees Fahrenheit.

Grace and Jaden jumped off the boat and splashed in the shallow water. Dad swam a while and then went back to the boat. He sat on deck taking notes in his notebook while keeping an eye on them. Nikos and Eleni were doing something on the boat as well. Daphne went to shore to count plants for her studies. Grace was glad she didn't ask for help, since it was cooler in the water.

Something brushed past Grace's foot. Probably Jaden trying to scare her. She treaded water and looked around. Her brother was 10 feet away, jumping from the sandy beach into the small waves as they splashed against the shore. Grace tried to look down into the water, but with the moving waves and the sparkling sun, she couldn't see much. Maybe it had been a fish. A small one. Totally not dangerous.

She tried to stand up. Her toes touched the sandy bottom.

Something grabbed her ankle!

Chapter Ten

SAVING THE DAY

Grace gasped and tried to shake it off, but it clung tightly. She splashed toward shore. The slimy thing kept its grip on her ankle. When the water was only knee-deep, she pulled up her leg and shook it. A piece of seaweed fell off and floated on the water for a moment before sinking.

"Honey?" Her father called from the boat. "Are you all right?"

Her dad and Jaden were staring at her. She felt herself blushing. "I'm fine. I just got caught on some seaweed. Everything's fine." She dove back into the water to hide her embarrassment. Jaden would tease her about that for certain.

Then she got an idea. She would have to take off her life jacket for a few minutes. And go a little farther from shore. But she wouldn't be doing anything that the grownups said was dangerous.

And if she scared herself a little, it would be worth it.

She set her life jacket safely on the beach and waded in the shallows. Once Jaden swam farther from shore, Grace swam close while his back was turned. She took a deep breath and dove under the water liked she'd learned in swim class. It was clear enough to see Jaden a few feet away. Grace kicked hard, stretched out a hand, and grabbed his ankle.

She could hear only a faint muffled sound from under the water. But the way Jaden kicked and splashed told her she'd surprised him. She let go and backed up to avoid getting kicked in the face. She rose to the surface grinning. "That time I got you," she said, laughing at Jaden's expression.

Grace swam back to land. She decided to walk along the shore, letting her feet sink into the wet sand, before she got back in the water. Maybe she could get more comfortable with swimming in the ocean. No, she knew she could, if she believed she could. But it would take some time. That was all right. She would try a little bit harder every day.

The wet sand squished between her toes. Sometimes a small wave came farther on shore, lapping over her feet. The cool water was a nice contrast to the hot air.

Something large sat at the edge of the water ahead. It was a dark, rounded dome a couple of feet long. Grace glanced at the boat to make sure she was still in clear sight. Her father waved.

She crept closer to the thing. Was it only a rock? A pillow that had fallen in the ocean?

Or was it alive – had she found a sea monster after all?

A wave pushed the thing farther onto shore. The brown, oval lump had legs and a head sticking out of it. A mouth opened and eyes seemed to look at her. It was alive! But this was no mysterious monster. It was a turtle, though bigger than any she'd seen before. Grace crouched a few feet away and watched it. Jaden would want to see it as well, but first she would enjoy a few minutes alone with this wild animal.

The turtle flapped a flipper. Its throat moved as it swallowed. The shiny black eyes closed.

Another wave washed over the turtle and pulled it a few feet out to sea. The turtle floated sideways but didn't try to swim. It seemed sick.

Grace jumped up and looked around for help. She spotted Daphne a few hundred feet away. Daphne worked with animals; she would know what to do. Grace called to her.

A few minutes later, Daphne, Eleni, Dad and Jaden had all gathered around the turtle. Dad held Jaden back so he wouldn't get too close.

As a small wave lifted the turtle, Daphne shifted it farther onto the beach. "A loggerhead sea turtle, female, I think. You're right, she looks sick. She should be more active, especially with people so close."

"Can you help her?" Grace asked.

"We can take her to a vet. I can't tell what's wrong. Maybe she swallowed plastic. To sea turtles, plastic bags look like a jellyfish, so they eat them. Then the plastic blocks their digestive tract. They slowly starve to death."

Grace and Jaden both exclaimed their horror.

"I've heard a lot of plastic gets dumped in the ocean," Dad said.

"Why would anyone do that?" Grace asked.

"Mostly by accident," Daphne said. "People drop their trash on the beach, or it gets blown away when they're not paying attention. Things fall off boats. That's why we make sure everything is stowed properly. Even garbage left far inland can make its way to the ocean. A plastic grocery bag caught in a bush in an empty lot might someday reach the sea. Thousands of animals are killed by plastic every year. Whales have died from swallowing too much garbage. Seals and sharks can get caught with plastic rings around their noses or necks."

"That's terrible!" Grace said. "Can't we do anything?"

"We certainly can," Daphne said. "We can use less plastic. We can make sure the plastic we use is properly recycled or thrown away. Some cities have banned plastic grocery bags, which is great. Even if your local store uses plastic bags, you can bring your own reusable cloth bag. The thing is, we all have to work together. Most of the damage comes not because people are cruel, but because they are careless."

Grace thought about that while Daphne stood and called instructions to Nikos on the boat. The sea turtle was strange-looking, and maybe scary if you didn't know what it was. But it was harmless. Other animals really could hurt people. But you could avoid going where a shark lived. The shark couldn't avoid living where people dumped garbage.

Nikos backed the boat close to shore. Daphne and Eleni each took hold of one side of the turtle's shell. The turtle's flippers flapped a couple of times as they lifted it. They waded into the water and lifted the turtle up to the side of the boat. Nikos grabbed the turtle and lowered it down to the deck.

Daphne called to Dad and the kids. "Hop in, and let's get this turtle to the doctor."

As they sailed toward help, Grace watched the turtle. Its shiny black eyes blinked. Its throat moved as it swallowed. Grace couldn't bear the thought that it might die.

A hand touched her shoulder. She glanced up at Daphne and asked, "Do you think she'll live?"

"I'll bet she will. I've seen turtles in worse shape survive once they had help. We're going to get this one to the animal doctor in time. In a few weeks, she'll be back swimming in the ocean."

Grace sighed in relief. "That's good. We won't be here to see it though."

Daphne squeezed her shoulder. "I'll see if I can get pictures to send you. You know, you asked what we could do to help. We're doing something right now. Because of you, this turtle has a chance at life. And if I'm right about it being female, she could go on to lay hundreds of eggs—hundreds of new little sea turtles."

Grace smiled. "I would love to see that! But what if some of those turtles get sick and don't have anyone to help?"

"Many projects in Greece try to protect and help sea turtles," Daphne said. "A lot of sea turtles nest on the beaches of Crete, and people also use the beaches. Some areas are now closed off to people. In other places, they put a cage over the nest to protect it. It's wonderful how aware people are today, and how many people care about protecting wildlife. We can make a difference. We're making a difference right now."

Grace nodded. Maybe someday she would come back to watch baby turtles hatch. Maybe when she grew up, she'd work with animals. She wanted to make a difference. But she didn't want to wait to do that. She'd learn all the ways to help animals. And she'd do them, starting now. The world was an amazing place, on land and in the ocean.

She'd help keep it that way. She believed it.

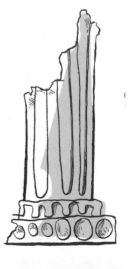

GRACE'S TRAVEL JOURNAL

In Greece, it's not polite to nod your head to say yes. You should say "Yes" out loud instead. Also, Greek people don't shake their heads to say no. Instead, nodding the head up a little means no. People shake hands when they meet children and adults.

The Greeks start work early in the morning. They end work at lunchtime! Some people may start work again at 5 p.m. and work late.

Being on time is not very important in Greece. If you are invited to someone's house, you should come 30 minutes late.

The Greeks are very friendly. They want you to eat more and stay longer. If you don't clean your plate, they'll ask you to keep eating. It's rude not to clean your plate. You are allowed to share with other people at the table, though.

Greek people like to dance and want their guests to join in. They have a lot of folk dances. Some of them are hard to learn, but for some you can just jump around and have fun!

Recipe

Horiatiki Salata: Greek Salad

Prep Time: about 15 minutes
Total Time: about 45 minutes
Serves: 4-6
4-5 large, ripe, tomatoes
1 cucumber
1 green bell pepper
1 large red onion
1/4 pound of Greek feta cheese, sliced or crumbled
1/4 cup extra virgin olive oil
1/4 cup red wine vinegar
1 teaspoon dried Greek oregano
salt and pepper to taste
1 dozen Greek olives, such as Kalamata or green Cretan olives
6-12 pickled pepperoncini peppers

Directions

Wash and dry the tomatoes, cucumber, and green pepper.

Ask an adult to help you with sharp knives. Cut the tomatoes into bite-sized pieces. Discard the core. Slice the cucumber into 1/4-inch slices. Cut the slices in half. Slice the pepper into rings. Discard the stem and seeds.

Remove the outer skin from the onion. Cut off the stem end and discard. Slice the onion into thin rings. Combine all the vegetables in a large salad bowl.

In a small bowl, mix together the olive oil, red wine vinegar, oregano, salt and pepper.

Pour this mixture over the salad and toss (mix lightly). For best results, let this sit for 30 minutes to blend the flavors.

Slice or crumble the feta cheese. Sprinkle it on top of the salad. Add the olives and pepperoncini. Serve.

Country Facts

Capital: Athens

Official Language: Greek

Population: About 10.8 million

Climate: Mild, with hot, dry summers and wet winters.

Famous people

Socrates, Plato, and Aristotle were famous philosophers. They all lived more than 2,200 years ago. They thought and wrote about how people should behave and what makes a person good. They also wrote about math and science. Plato founded the Academy in Athens. This was the first place for advanced education in the Western world.

Hippocrates, a Greek doctor, was born in 460 BCE. He is considered the founder of Western medicine.

Sappho is a famous woman poet who was born in 610 BCE. She is admired for her beautiful writing. Other Greek poets from about the same time were Archilochus and Alcaeus.

Events and Holidays

Greek Independence Day is March 25. The land now called Greece was controlled by the Turks for almost 400 years. In 1821, a revolution started. It ended in 1829 and Greece became an independent country. People celebrate the date with parades and marches. Children march in traditional Greek costumes, carrying Greek flags.

Easter is an important holiday. On Good Friday, people carry candles in a procession. A ceremony takes place on Saturday and bells are rung. Easter Sunday is celebrated with religious services and a feast of roast lamb. People hold battles where eggs, dyed red, are hit together. Whoever's egg cracks the least is supposed to have good luck.

Landmarks

Delphi: Delphi was the center of the ancient Greek world. The Delphi Oracle gave prophecies to people who asked for advice. People now visit the remains of a theater, stadium, gymnasium, and other sites. A museum holds many ancient treasures.

Knossos: The Minoans built a civilization starting about 4,000 years ago. Knossos was their capital city. It was excavated and partly rebuilt in the early 1900s. It is Crete's most visited tourist attraction. It is also one of the most important archaeology sites in the world.

The Acropolis: A city of temples, dedicated to the gods. It was the most important ancient site in the Western world. It has many ancient monuments. The most famous is the Parthenon, dedicated to the goddess Athena. The Acropolis was most active in the fifth century BCE. Many tourists now visit from nearby Athens.

Now and Then

Long ago, people asked advice from the Delphi Oracle. She sat in the Temple of Apollo to give her answers. The Temple fell into ruins centuries ago. It doesn't even look like a building anymore. Once it would have been a beautiful and mysterious place.

Drawing of the Delphi Oracle:

Temple to Apollo, where the oracle sat:

Discussion Questions

1. Why might people want to know the future?
2. How could believing something help it become true?
3. Do you think laws should protect places like Delphi, or should people be able to take things they find at ancient sites? Who should own objects that were abandoned long ago?
4. Is there power in music? How could a song or story influence someone?
5. Daphne says the moral to the story of Orpheus is that you shouldn't give up too soon. Can you think of an example where that would be good advice?
6. Is it worth preparing for disasters? Is your area at risk for certain types of disasters? What could your family do to get ready?
7. When Daphne tells the story of Perseus, Ariadne, and the Minotaur, she says, "Being smart is often more important than being tough." What does this mean? Do you agree? Why or why not?

Vocabulary Words

Do you know what these words mean? Write a story using as many of them as you can.

acrobat

afloat

archaeologist

artifact

biologist

column

deckhand

excavate

formation

labyrinth

marble

metaphor

mortal

overboard

prophecy

shrine

stalactites

stalagmites

stow

venomous

Websites to Visit

www.unep.org/regionalseas/marinelitter/kids/default.asp

www.bbc.co.uk/schools/primaryhistory/ancient_greeks

www.ducksters.com/history/ancient_greece.php

About the Author

M. M. Eboch writes fiction and nonfiction for all ages. Writing as Chris Eboch, her novels for young people include *The Genie's Gift*, a middle eastern fantasy; *The Eyes of Pharaoh*, a mystery in ancient Egypt; and the Haunted series, which starts with *The Ghost on the Stairs*. As M. M. Eboch, her books include nonfiction and the fictionalized biographies *Jesse Owens: Young Record Breaker* and *Milton Hershey: Young Chocolatier*. You can find out more about her at www.chriseboch.com.

About the Illustrator

Sarah Horne studied Illustration at Falmouth College of Arts, England, graduating in 2001. Sarah now specializes in funny inky illustration and text for young fiction and picture books. She also works on book covers, magazine and newspaper editorials and in Advertising. She loves music, painting, color, photography, film, scratchy jazz and a good cup of coffee.

Sarah lives on a hill in London, UK.